Mermaid
in the

To Oma Peetoom, in memoriam;
and for Sam and Marti
L.P.

FIRST FLIGHT® is a registered trademark of Fitzhenry & Whiteside.
Text copyright © 2006 by Laura Peetoom
Illustrations copyright © 2006 by Eugenie Fernandes

Published in Canada by Fitzhenry & Whiteside,
195 Allstate Parkway, Markham, Ontario L3R 4T8

Published in the United States by Fitzhenry & Whiteside,
311 Washington Street, Brighton, Massachusetts 02135

www.fitzhenry.ca   godwit@fitzhenry.ca

10 9 8 7 6 5 4 3 2 1

Library and Archives Canada Cataloguing in Publication
Peetoom, Laura
Mermaid in the bathtub / Laura Peetoom ; illustrated by Eugenie Fernandes.
ISBN 1-55041-362-7
I. Fernandes, Eugenie, 1943- II. Title.
PS8631.E38M47 2006   jC813'.6   C2005-907256-3

U.S. Publisher Cataloging-in-Publication Data
(Library of Congress Standards)

Peetoom, Laura.
Mermaid in the bathtub / Laura Peetoom ; illustrated by Eugenie Fernandes.
[40] p. : col. ill. ; cm.
Summary: When Sam and Marina spot a mermaid in their parents' fish shop,
they take her home and hide her from the adults, who think she's just
a fish to cook. Only their father's old friend from Turkey recognizes
the mermaid, and the old lady has an idea.
ISBN 1-55041-362-7
1. Mermaids — Fiction — Juvenile literature.
I. Fernandes, Eugenie II. Title. [E] dc22   PZ7.P448Me   2006

Fitzhenry & Whiteside acknowledges with thanks the Canada Council for the Arts,
and the Ontario Arts Council for their support of our publishing program. We
acknowledge the financial support of the Government of Canada through the Book
Publishing Industry Development Program (BPIDP) for our publishing activities.

Design by Wycliffe Smith Design Inc.
Printed in Canada

A First Flight® Level Four Reader

Mermaid in the Bathtub

by Laura Peetoom
Illustrated by Eugenie Fernandes

Fitzhenry & Whiteside

CHAPTER ONE

That Can't Be Her!

"What does she look like again?" asked
Sam.

"She has dark brown hair, round cheeks,
and really warm eyes—Hala Aisha is very
beautiful," said Dad. He strained to see
above the crowd at the airport arrivals
gate.

"Calm down, Dad," Marina said, pulling
on his shirt.

Sam and Marina had heard about Hala
Aisha all their lives. When their father was
a little boy in Turkey, Hala Aisha lived
next door. She had been very kind to him

after his mother died. Even though he was grown up and living in Canada, he still wrote a letter to Hala Aisha every week. He talked about her a lot, too. Now she was coming for a visit at last.

"Just wait till you taste her cooking," said Dad. "Did I tell you she's a great cook?"

"Only about a million times," said Sam.

"Great cook, great storyteller, great singer...," said Marina, counting off on her fingers.

"And the soccer games—don't forget those," added Sam.

Marina counted off "great goalkeeper" on her fourth finger, then moved to her thumb. "And she smells good when she hugs you," she finished.

Dad got that dreamy look on his face again.

"Like spices and flowers," he said.

Sam and Marina pretended to gag. But they were looking forward to Hala Aisha's visit, too.

Last summer had been hard. Sam and Marina had spent many hot, boring days

stuck in the house and the yard. Their parents owned a fish market around the corner, where they worked all day. With no one to supervise them, the children were not allowed to go far from home by themselves.

Maybe this summer would be different. Sam and Marina would go to the playground and the pool with Hala Aisha. They would take trips downtown. Hala Aisha would make treats for them. She would help them with projects. They would have friends over. It would be the best summer ever.

Sam and Marina watched the arrivals gate almost as eagerly as their dad. Only Mom was not watching. She had her nose in a book, as usual.

The doors slid open, and a man and child walked through. A few people greeted them with hugs and shouts. The doors closed, then opened again. A stream of people poured into the terminal. The crowd broke apart as relatives and friends greeted one another, gathered their baggage, and left.

As the crowd lessened, Sam and Marina stood at the railing and stared at each new arrival. They searched for dark brown hair, round cheeks, warm eyes, and lots of energy. As the flood of arrivals turned into a trickle, Sam and Marina's parents joined them at the railing. The doors shut with a hiss. They slid open again as the last few arrivals came through.

"There she is!" said Dad.

Marina looked up. Mom had tucked her book under her arm. Dad had a strange expression on his face. It was sad, happy, and just a little bit scared. It made Marina feel funny.

Sam poked her with his elbow. An old, old lady, shaped like a big, bumpy pear, stood in front of them. She wore a black scarf over her head. Her face was wrinkly and saggy. She held a photograph in her hand. She looked at it, and then she looked at them. She held it out. It was their last year's vacation picture.

"Hello, Sam?" said the old lady. She pointed first to the picture, then at Sam.

Sam grabbed Marina's hand. "This is

Marina," he said.

The old lady nodded. "Marina?... I very happy to meet," she said.

At least, that's what Marina *thought* she said.

And then her dad hugged the old lady and burst into a flood of Turkish. He pushed Sam and Marina and their mom forward to be hugged, too.

Sam and Marina waited with the old lady while Mom and Dad went to fetch her suitcases. The children looked at each other silently. All their plans for the summer whirled and swirled and drained away.

"She's old," whispered Sam.

"She's *ancient*," whispered Marina. "She is *nothing* like the way Dad described her!"

"So much for summer," whispered Sam.

"This *can't* be Hala Aisha," whispered Marina.

But she knew it was. Dad had been right about one thing. Marina had first noticed it during the hug. She noticed it again as she and her brother followed the old lady out of the airport, across the roadway, and into the car park. She noticed it as Dad stowed the old lady's suitcases in the trunk. She couldn't ignore it when she squished in between Sam and Hala Aisha in the back seat of the car.

Hala Aisha *did* smell of spices and flowers.

Long-ago, dusty spices.

Very old, dried-up flowers.

CHAPTER TWO

Hot and Bothered

"I'm HOT," complained Marina. "I wish we could go to the pool or the park—at least there's grass there."

The kids were sitting on the front porch. Their Popsicles were melting faster than they could eat them.

Sam shook his head. "Mom said we couldn't leave Hala Aisha," he said.

"BO-ring!" said Marina. "And it's so unfair." She pushed her Popsicle stick between two floor boards and watched it disappear. "Couldn't she come with us? She could sit with all the other old ladies on the benches."

"I guess so. But...," Sam sighed.

Marina sighed, too. It was all so complicated.

During the past two weeks, the old lady had spent hours in the living room looking at photo albums. She compared pictures of Sam and Marina as babies with old pictures of their father in the album she'd brought with her.

She spent a lot of time in the kitchen, too, with a big knife in her hand. The stuff she chopped and rolled looked and smelled strange, but their dad loved it. So did Mom.

She kept urging the kids to try. Sam and Marina refused. They were suspicious of any new food, especially when it was wrapped in boiled leaves.

When she wasn't cooking or looking at pictures, Hala Aisha just kind of sat there in Marina's bedroom. Marina was bunking with Sam.

"Behold the ancient Galapagos Tortoise," whispered Sam one night, as they passed the open door on their way to bed. Like Mom, he read a lot.

"Ancient *Auntie* Galapagos Tortoise to you," said Marina, and giggled.

Dad was coming out of the bathroom just then, and he overheard them. He frowned.

"Don't be rude," he said. "Why don't you go in and talk to her?"

"But, Dad," said Marina, "we don't know what to say."

"You're not trying hard enough. What happened to the Turkish I taught you last winter? And Hala Aisha knows some English. She's been studying for months. You could help her practice."

Sam and Marina exchanged looks. It wasn't just language that was the problem. If she were a kid, they might have thought Hala Aisha was shy. But she wasn't a kid, or even the kind of grownup they were used to. They had no clue what to do with her.

But they tried. They pointed at things—furniture, kitchen tools, plants in the garden—and said the names for them, which the old lady repeated. When they got tired of that, Hala Aisha showed them the English book she'd borrowed from a friend back home in Turkey.

"Where is the lavatory?" Sam read. "I am in need of a chemist."

Marina burst out laughing. Sam found another page. "I want a car with a roomy boot," he read, this time in a funny voice. "Have you a lorry for hire? Where is the petrol station?"

He kept reading bits from the book until Marina was rolling on the floor, holding her stomach. "Stop, stop! I can't take any more!" she gasped, and Sam turned to give the book back to Hala Aisha. She was gone, back to the kitchen.

And after that, they pretty much avoided one another—like they were doing now.

Marina sighed again. "I can't stay on the porch another minute," she said. "Let's find the Ancient Auntie and give it a try."

"Okay," said Sam. They went inside.

The old lady wasn't in the kitchen, but they could hear splashing sounds outside. They peeked out the window. There she was, bent over the big plastic tub that Mom used to collect rainwater for the garden.

"Is the washing machine broken?" asked Sam.

"I guess so," said Marina. The old lady pulled a wet black thing—it looked like a stocking—from the water. She wrung it out and pinned it up, right next to the huge white thing already flapping on the clothesline.

"What's *that?*" wondered Sam.

"Underpants," said Marina, "I think."

"Wow. Must be size *dinosaur!*" Sam said. Marina put her hand over her mouth to keep the giggles in.

The kids watched as Hala Aisha hung up the rest of her laundry. When she finished, the old lady sat on a chair and put her feet in the tub. Sam and Marina had never seen her legs before. They were pale and hairy, and they were covered with blue lumps and squiggles. She lifted her feet from the water and waved them in the air. The heels were cracked, and the toes were crooked.

"Scary," whispered Sam.

Marina pushed open the screen door. "Well, here goes," she said.

"Hala Aisha," she started.

The old lady looked up and smiled.

"Will you take us to the park?" asked Sam.

Sam ran around in a tight circle, pretending to kick a ball. Marina tried to mime being on a swing. The Ancient Auntie watched them, still smiling but puzzled.

"Um, you know, grass, *les arbres...* um..." From somewhere deep in his brain, the Turkish word for "trees" popped up. "*Ağaçlar?*"

Marina fanned her face with her hand. "It's cooler there," she said, temptingly.

The old lady fanned her wrinkled face with her hand, too.

"I don't think she's getting it," said Sam.

The old lady said something in Turkish, pointing to their feet and then to her tub.

"No *thanks*," the kids said, at exactly the same time.

With the fingers of one hand, the old woman made a circle and lifted it to her lips.

"I think she wants a drink," said Marina.

The kids went back into the kitchen. Sam put ice in three glasses, and Marina poured the lemonade.

"You know, she'd feel cooler if she didn't wear black all the time," said Marina.

"You're wearing white, and you're still hot," Sam pointed out.

Marina frowned. Sam was always fair, even when Marina didn't want him to be. She flounced out with her own glass, leaving Sam to carry the other two.

The old woman took a sip and looked at the children's hot, grumpy faces for a while. She said something in Turkish—Sam thought he heard the words for "supper" and "fish." Then she waved them away.

"She wants us to go get something for supper," said Sam.

"I guess hamburgers and fries are too much to hope for," said Marina.

"That's what you get when there's a fish market in the family," said Sam.

They let the front door bang shut behind them.

CHAPTER THREE

Something's Not Fishy Around Here

It was a relief to get inside the fish market. Above the door, the air conditioner hummed and blew. In the window, the fish lay like cool rainbows in a sky of ice. It felt good just to look at them.

Nick, the helper, was on the phone.

"Probably talking to his girlfriend," said Marina loudly.

"Which one?" said Sam, even louder. Nick waved them away, frowning. The kids helped themselves to pop from the cooler, then headed for the backroom.

"Watch out," called Nick, as the kids

opened the door. "A shipment just came in, and your folks are going crazy!"

It *was* busy. The backroom smelled like diesel. Two delivery guys were unloading stuff from the back of a truck.

Mom came toward them, a big crate in her arms. "What are you two doing here?" she asked crossly. "You know you're supposed to stay with the Ancient—er, Hala Aisha!" She plunked the crate down on the stack beside the door. Some ice fell to the floor.

"She told us to...," began Marina, but Sam poked her with his elbow.

"Look!" he said in a strangled whisper. He pointed. Marina's eyes grew round and her mouth dropped open.

"You don't have to look so shocked," said Mom. "We've had bigger fish than that in here."

Sam and Marina stared at each other, and then at their mother. Couldn't she see?

"But it's a—ow!" gasped Marina. Sam had stepped on her toe.

"Can we take it home?" he asked quickly.

"Sure," said Mom. Now it was her turn to look surprised. The children always complained when there was fish for supper. "I'll ask Nick to clean it."

"No!" Marina looked wild.

"You know how the Ancient Auntie likes doing it herself," said Sam quickly.

"Don't call her that," said Mom. She went to get some sacking. Marina reached out a trembling finger and touched the pale cheek in the crate.

"Don't touch it! Act normal!" snapped Sam in a hoarse whisper.

Mom returned, made a neat bundle of the thing and tucked it under her children's arms.

"Hurry home," she said sternly. "And give this to Hala Aisha as soon as you get there, okay? It's too big to fit in the fridge in one piece."

"We'll hurry," promised Sam carefully.

They went out the delivery door into the back alley.

"What are we going to do?" asked Marina.

"We'll hurry, just like we promised," said Sam. "And hope that it's still alive."

"I don't understand how Mom could think this was a fish," said Marina.

"Me neither," said Sam.

"Do you think it's magic?" asked Marina.

Sam didn't answer. The sack-wrapped bundle was awkward to carry. It took a lot of concentration to hold it and still walk fast.

A couple of cats were sniffing around some garbage cans. They lifted their noses when Sam and Marina came by, then ran after them. They circled the kids' ankles, meowing and rubbing. Marina stumbled.

"Hey! Watch it!" cried Sam.

"It's these darn cats!" said Marina.

Just as they came out of the alley onto their street, a man walked by with a dog on a leash. The dog lifted his nose and barked. It was a big dog and a big bark. Marina screamed and dropped her end of the bundle. A corner of the sacking unwrapped itself. The cats pounced.

"Down! Down!" the man shouted.

Marina dropped to the ground.

"No, not you!" cried the man.

The dog barked; the cats yowled and hissed. Sam knew he had to get out of there. He didn't think about how heavy it was. He just gathered up the whole bundle and started running.

The cats ran after him. The dog jumped again, pulling his leash right out of the man's hand. Then the dog bounded after the cats, his leash trailing behind him.

Marina jumped up and ran after the dog. So did the man. They snatched at the leash at the same time, and their heads bonked together. But Marina had caught it. The dog yipped and strained against the leash, pulling Marina's arms almost out of their sockets. Her head was throbbing. She

felt like a character in a Saturday morning cartoon.

"Are you all right?" asked the man.

"I'm fine. I'm fine," Marina said quickly. She shoved the leash in the man's hands and ran after Sam.

"I'm sorry about your fish!" the man called after her. "Let me buy you another!"

"That's okay!" Marina called back, and kept running.

Marina didn't stop when she caught up with Sam. She ran right past him and up their porch steps, in time to open the door.

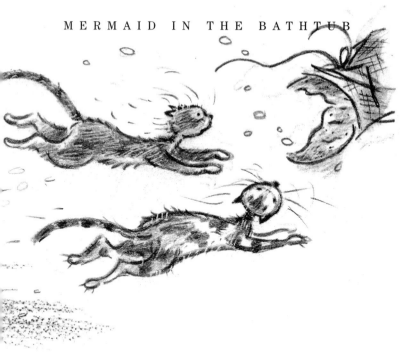

"Go see where the Ancient Auntie is," panted Sam.

Marina went straight to the kitchen. The old woman was still outside on the deck, sitting there with her feet in the plastic tub. Marina ran back to Sam.

"All clear," she said. "Let's take it upstairs."

Together they brought the bundle up the stairs and into the bathroom. Marina filled the bathtub with cool water. Sam hoisted the limp bundle into it. They carefully removed the sacking. Then they waited.

The mermaid's hair spread out and filled the tub all around her. A scent like tears filled the room.

Marina sighed. The ache in her head and arms went away.

"Don't they live in the sea?" asked Sam.

Marina nodded. "And the sea is salty— I'll be right back."

Marina went down to the kitchen and poked around the cupboards, looking for the big box of salt Mom used to shrivel up garden slugs. She hoisted herself onto the counter and stood up to reach the cupboard above the stove. There it was. As she was getting down, Marina glanced out the kitchen window. The chair on the deck was empty.

Marina ran to the living room. No Ancient Auntie. Alarm bells were going off in Marina's head. She raced up the stairs, just in time to see the old woman disappear into the bathroom.

"No!" Marina screamed. She ran to the bathroom. Sam was guarding the tub with outspread arms.

"It's not a fish! You can't cook her!" he

was yelling.

The Ancient Auntie was talking fast and loud. She turned around, grabbed Marina and gave her a little shake.

"*Bu bir Denizkizi!*" she said, then rushed out of the room and down the stairs. Marina started after her.

"Give me the salt!" said Sam fiercely.

"But I've got to stop her!" wailed Marina. "She's getting her knife! She thinks it's dinner!"

Sam grabbed the box. The salt hissed into the tub like a dry waterfall. Sam plunged his hands in the water and swirled them about. The mermaid stirred.

"She's alive!" said Marina.

The mermaid's eyes opened.

A Tail Tale

Sam and Marina stared and stared. They didn't hear the old woman coming back up the stairs. They didn't see what she had in her hands. They only dragged their gaze away when she said, "Come. See."

The old woman was sitting down with a photo album spread open on her lap. She pointed to a photo of two figures in the sea. They were so small and far away, it was hard to see who they were. "Hala Aisha," she said, pointing to the one on the left. She pointed to the one on the right. "Friend."

Then she pointed to the bathtub.

"You were friends with a mermaid?" breathed Marina.

The old lady nodded and began to tell them a story.

Huh, thought Sam in the middle of it. *I guess I learned more from Dad than I thought—Hala Aisha's speaking Turkish, but I understand every word.*

We shouldn't have made fun of that English book, thought Marina at the same time. *Hala Aisha's English is really very good, after all.*

The old lady told them how she had grown up in a village by the sea. She loved to be in the water, even though she couldn't swim. One day, a strange girl swam up to her—from the sea, not the shore. She swam around for a while, smiling and splashing. Hala Aisha moved her arms in the water the way the strange girl was doing. Then she looked under the water to see what the girl was doing with her legs. That is when Hala Aisha saw it wasn't a girl at all.

"Weren't you scared?" asked Sam.

The old lady smiled. "No. She was so lively and glad, you see."

All summer long, the two played and swam in the waves. Then summer ended. Hala Aisha had to go back to school. The two friends exchanged gifts and said good-bye.

"And she told me her name," said the old lady. "Listen."

Hala Aisha made a sound like a gurgle and a shriek, with a song in the middle. They heard the sound again, and turned to look. It was the mermaid. Her eyes shone, and she clapped her hands. She sang. She bubbled. She splashed. Soon Sam, Marina, Hala Aisha, and the bathroom were all soaking wet.

Sam got a stack of towels from the closet in the hall, and they all mopped up. Then they dried themselves off.

"I'm glad she's feeling better," said Marina, "but what do we do now?"

Sam had already been thinking about this. "We'll tell Mom and Dad," he said. "When they know what she is, they'll *have* to let us keep her."

Hala Aisha looked doubtful.

"I don't know about that," said Marina.

The phone rang, and Sam ran to answer it. Hala Aisha began to comb out Marina's damp, tangled hair. She pulled the comb slowly, and her hands on Marina's head were gentle.

"It doesn't hurt when you do it, Hala Aisha," said Marina shyly.

Sam came back and taped a sign he'd made to the bathroom door. It read, *Do Not Disturb*.

"Mom and Dad will be a little late tonight," he said. "Let's have supper all ready. After supper, we can show them the mermaid."

Hala Aisha bundled up the wet towels.

"No fish, no dinner," she said. "What do I cook?"

"Hamburgers!" the children shouted.

Sam got the patties out of the freezer and showed Hala Aisha how to work the barbecue. Marina helped her slice tomatoes and wash lettuce. Then both kids set the table. While they worked, they made plans.

"Do you think there might be a spare lobster tank at the market?" Sam asked Marina.

"Maybe I could ask for one of those really big aquariums for my birthday," she suggested. "What do mermaids eat, anyway?"

"Fish," said Hala Aisha. "Lobsters, mussels, smelts…"

"Hey! It's a good thing there's a fish market in the family!" said Sam.

CHAPTER FIVE

Mermaid Surprise

"Smells delicious," said Mom, when she and Dad came home. "But what happened to the fish?"

"We'll tell you later," said Sam.

"Is there time for a shower?" asked Dad, starting up the stairs.

"No!" cried the kids. "Just use the downstairs bathroom to wash up," suggested Marina quickly.

During supper, Hala Aisha asked Marina if she wanted more milk.

"No, thanks," said Marina.

"Marina!" said Dad.

"What?" said Marina. "I used my manners."

"You understand Turkish!" said Dad. He looked delighted.

Marina stared at him. "What do you mean? That was plain English."

Mom shook her head. "It's amazing how fast kids pick up languages—she's not even aware of it," she said to Dad.

"No—it's those Turkish lessons I gave them last winter," Dad answered, and while they argued, Marina glanced at Sam. Sam looked at Hala Aisha, and the old lady smiled back at both of them, one finger across her lips.

Dad was right, Sam thought. *Hala Aisha does have warm eyes.*

Mom made coffee, Dad and Hala Aisha started talking about the old country, and the fish upstairs was almost forgotten. Then, while Sam and Marina were doing the dishes, they heard a scream. They raced upstairs on Dad's heels.

"You take care of this," Mom told Dad, pointing. "I'll be in the garden." She glowered at Sam and Marina as she passed by.

"Kids, what have you been...?" Dad's voice trailed off as he went into the bathroom. Sam and Marina followed him. "Is this the fish you brought home from the market?" he asked incredulously.

Then Sam and Marina looked into the bathtub. The mermaid *did* look more like a fish than she had before. She was curled up so tightly that her tail covered her face, and she was lying on most of her hair. But still, she didn't look like any kind of fish the kids had ever seen. They didn't know what to say.

It looked like Dad didn't either. His face turned red and his mouth opened and shut a few times. "Just like a fish's," Marina said later.

Dad let out his breath with a whoosh and sat down.

"Kids, you couldn't possibly be thinking of keeping a dead fish as a...a...as some kind of pet, could you?" he pleaded. "So there must be some other reason you have this fish here. Please tell me what it is."

"Uh...," said Sam.

"Well...," began Marina.

Like a gift from heaven, Hala Aisha came to their rescue. She beckoned to Dad from the bathroom doorway and shut the door behind him.

The mermaid uncovered her face and stared up at them with big, frightened eyes.

"All clear," whispered Marina.

"Shhh!" hissed Sam. He was listening hard, his ear pressed to the bathroom door. "She's saying the fish is a gift for a new friend... Dad's asking where they met... Hala Aisha's saying we introduced them... Whew!" Sam grinned. "She's *good.*"

"I don't get it," said Marina, shaking her head. "First Mom, then that man in the street, and now Dad can't see her. I'm not complaining or anything, but why can't they see the mermaid?"

Sam had already been thinking about this. "I think most people see only what they expect to see," he told Marina.

"Maybe," said Marina, "but *I* think it's magic. Just like the talking."

Later, everyone but Hala Aisha went swimming. Mom brought all her lotions and potions, and Dad brought his shaving things, since neither of them would be using the bathroom in the morning.

"I buy and sell and handle fish all day long," said Dad, "and I'm happy to eat them for dinner. But I draw the line at sharing my morning shower with a fish."

On the way home from the pool, Mom gave Sam and Marina a little lecture.

"I know it's Hala Aisha who wanted to keep the fish," she said, "but I'm holding you responsible. Make sure it gets to her friend or whatever it is she wants. When I get home from the market tomorrow, I don't want to see any more fish in my bathtub. Is that clear?"

The kids nodded. "You won't see a thing," promised Sam.

A Fishy, Noisy, Expensive Secret

"Now what?" said Marina, right after breakfast the next day.

Sam had already been thinking of another hiding place. "There's that plastic tub on the deck," he said. "We could put it in your room, Marina. That is, if..." He looked at Hala Aisha, and the old lady nodded. He ran downstairs to get it.

It took Mom's watering can and many trips between the bathroom and Marina's room to fill the plastic tub. It was just big enough to cover the mermaid's fishy part, if she curled up a little. The salt box was empty.

"You can get sea salt at the health food store," said Marina. "That would be nicer than regular salt, don't you think?"

So Sam and Marina got their money and went around the corner to the health food store, leaving Hala Aisha in charge of the mermaid. They scooped up a big bagful.

"Starting an aquarium?" joked the clerk. Then she told them the price.

"Keeping a mermaid is going to be expensive," said Marina to Sam, fingering her empty wallet on the way home. As they came up the front steps, they could hear lots of noise inside. Their neighbor, Miss McVitie, was standing on her porch.

"I'm back!" she called. "What a trip!"

"Not now!" Sam groaned to Marina.

Miss McVitie liked to

talk—and talk and talk and talk. She was impossible to interrupt. She'd been away for ages, visiting her relatives in Scotland. So now she had even more to say than usual. She trotted down her steps and hurried toward them.

"I lost my glasses in Loch Ness; I had a wee accident in Edinburgh; and—"

"Nice to see you, Miss McVitie! Gotta go!" said Marina, and pulled her brother inside. Sometimes Sam was just too polite. She closed the door firmly behind them.

Upstairs, the mermaid was crying and clutching her tummy—well, the place where her person part met her fish part, anyway.

"What's wrong?" asked Marina.

"She is hungry," said Hala Aisha. "Get some fish."

"Try to keep her quiet," begged Sam.

When the kids came outside, Miss McVitie was waiting on their porch.

"Your mother's a slyboots. She never said a word about the *bairn!* Let me help. I used to be a nanny, you know. I know all about these things. It's probably colic. I'll just come in a minute and make a cup of tea for your mother, and then—"

"Thanks, Miss McVitie. Maybe later," said Sam. "Will you excuse us, please?"

"What was she talking about?" said Marina, as they hurried down the street.

"I don't know," said Sam.

They burst through the market door.

"Smelts, please, Nick!" panted Sam.

"Lots of them!" added Marina

Nick scooped up a big bagful.

"I thought you guys didn't like fish," he said.

"Hala Aisha told us to get it," said Sam. They ran all the way home. Miss McVitie was gone, thank goodness.

"Shouldn't we cook them?" asked Marina, handing the bag to Hala Aisha.

They watched as the mermaid gobbled the little silvery fish, one after another, smacking and slurping.

"There's no fire in the sea," Hala Aisha pointed out.

"I guess not," said Sam, feeling sick.

The mermaid stopped eating and let out a shockingly big burp. Then she handed

the bag of smelts—what was left of them—
to Hala Aisha, laid her head on her arms,
and went to sleep. The sudden silence
made their ears ring.

"Keeping a mermaid is going to be
expensive and noisy," said Marina. *And
tough to keep secret*, said a little voice
inside her. She pushed the pesky thought
away.

"And fishy," Sam added later. Because
of course they had to have the rest of the
smelts for dinner.

And a lot of work, Marina discovered
still later. Sam was snoring, but Marina
was too excited to sleep. She listened to
Mom and Dad getting ready for bed.

"Where did these long red hairs come
from?" she heard Mom ask Dad from the
bathroom. "That ancient auntie of yours
doesn't have a wig, does she?"

"Don't call her that," Dad answered.

We'll have to vacuum every day,
thought Marina. Then she fell asleep.

Mermaid Frolics

Next morning, Sam and Marina carried the
mermaid into the bathroom and put her in
the tub. She stretched out with a sigh.

"You can be in here for a while every
day," Sam promised, "while Mom and Dad
are at work."

*Even a bathtub is small for a creature
that's used to an ocean,* said a little voice
inside him. He pushed the pesky thought
away.

Having a mermaid around was fishy and
risky and all those things. But it was fun,

too. Marina loved to comb the mermaid's hair. It was thick and springy. Each strand was like the thinnest rubber band. The mermaid kept wetting it, and when Marina cleaned her comb later, she found out why. When the hair dried, it became crunchy.

Sam tried to learn the mermaid's language, but it seemed to need a different kind of air than what came out of his lungs. To repeat her name properly—at least, he thought it was her name—Sam had to take a mouthful of water first. So he just called her Lyra. The mermaid seemed happy with that.

After two days of eating and sleeping, Lyra got restless. When they carried her between the bathroom and Hala Aisha's room, the mermaid wriggled energetically as she looked around, pointing and squealing with excitement. Soon, her curiosity got the better of them all. She flipped out of Sam and Marina's arms and flapped her way to the top of the stairs before they could stop her.

She was pretty startled when she bumped to the bottom, but she wasn't hurt.

"It's lucky her tail is slippery," said Marina. "She went down like a toboggan!"

They discovered that if Lyra wiggled her tail while the kids held her up by her arms, they could get around pretty well. So they gave her a tour. Sam found an undersea special on TV, and Lyra got excited. She pounded the screen and made such a loud keening noise that Sam quickly turned it off.

Hala Aisha helped her into the kitchen, to distract her with a couple of smelts. It worked—for a while. Though she shivered in the cold air, Lyra loved the little light in the fridge. She kept opening and shutting the door, and laughing. But after a few minutes of that, she lay down on the floor, screeching and patting her tail.

Sam held his hands over his ears. Marina wanted to cry. But Hala Aisha knew what to do. She emptied a spray bottle of window cleaner and washed it out. Then she refilled it with cool salt water. She sprayed the mermaid all over, and soon Lyra was happy again.

After that, they spent some time downstairs every day. Hala Aisha suggested they take the mermaid outside as well. They were all spending too much time indoors, she said.

Sam brought the small tub downstairs again and set it up on the deck. They were shielded by trees on all sides but one. Only Miss McVitie's place had a window that overlooked their garden. And luckily Miss McVitie was terribly near-sighted.

"A new dog, too?" she called, squinting down at them in the middle of Lyra's sea-animal impressions. "It barks just like a seal!"

They couldn't stop laughing. Hala Aisha laughed so hard, she got the hiccups.

Though it was fun doing things with Lyra, activities seemed to make her hungry. Sam and Marina brought her salmon, mahi mahi, oysters, scallops—and then had to pretend to like seafood themselves.

"I told you Hala Aisha was a great cook," said Dad. "She turned you into seafood lovers!"

Then one night the neighbors had barbecued chicken. The smell drifted through the trees, over the fence, and through the kitchen screen door. Even Dad left some fried whitefish on his plate.

"You know," he joked, "fish market owners are allowed to eat other things, too. There's a butcher shop right next to the fish market. I'm sure they would appreciate a little business."

So Sam and Marina asked for an advance on their allowance and went to the grocery store. The frozen fish was awfully expensive, so they bought one can each of tuna, salmon, and sardines. Lyra refused them.

"She really doesn't like cooked stuff," said Sam.

"I saw dried shrimp at the Asian grocery when Mom sent me there for Tiger

Balm," said Marina.

The dried shrimp was cheaper than the frozen kind. They had enough money for dried squid and cuttlefish and a bag of toasted seaweed, too. Mrs. Whan gave them an odd look when they paid for it.

"How's Eddie, Mrs. Whan?" asked Sam. "Is he going to camp this year?" He knew Mrs. Whan's son a little—he was in the grade below Marina, and Sam had been his reading buddy the year before. So he chatted with Mrs. Whan about Eddie until Marina was safely out the door with the supplies.

Lyra tossed the shrimp back like popcorn. She loved the seaweed, too, nibbling it like potato chips. But she sniffed the other things suspiciously and handed them back. Then she cried, because she was still hungry. Sam and Marina understood. Popcorn and potato chips don't make a meal, even if they are delicious.

"I guess we'll just have to go back to eating Lyra's leftovers," said Marina glumly.

Leftovers. An idea began to form in

Sam's mind. At the market there was a big barrel that held the scraps from the day's work. If they said it was for someone else…

Off they went, back to the market. They asked Nick to give them everything but the yucky insides of things. They said it was for Hala Aisha's friend.

"That friend must be a seal or something," said Nick. "She eats a lot of weird stuff."

"She's a mermaid," said Sam truthfully. Marina giggled.

Nick winked at her. "Sure, Sam," he said.

The day after, though, Mom caught them going out the shop door with their bag of scraps. She started asking questions, and they had to come up with answers. It was agony for Sam, who prided himself on always telling the truth.

"That friend you're talking about—how did they meet?" Mom asked. "The Ancient Auntie hardly ever goes out."

"Don't call her that!" said Marina.

"We brought her home with us," said Sam.

"What?! I told you, *never*—"

"Hala Aisha was there," said Sam. He was looking desperate.

Marina helped him out. "We were at the library, you see," she said. Mom loved the library. "And—"

"And we're really sorry, Mom, but it turned out okay, didn't it?" said Sam. Then he added quickly, "Wait till you see the book I got. Did you know that Aisha was one of the wives of the prophet Muhammad? Do you think Hala Aisha was named after her?"

Mom got all interested in that and in the book Sam was reading, just as Sam had hoped. She didn't forget, though. At bedtime, the kids heard her telling Dad about Hala Aisha's friend.

"What if Dad talks to Hala Aisha?" whispered Sam in a panic.

"No problem. I filled her in," said Marina.

The next morning, Mom asked, "So, how about we have this friend of your auntie's for supper sometime?"

"No!" said Marina, shocked.

Sam explained hastily, "She doesn't like people much. Just kids. And old people."

"When does Hala Aisha see her, then?" Mom persisted.

"Every day," said Sam.

"When you're at the shop," said Marina helpfully.

Sam groaned.

"What?" whispered Marina.

"You'll see," Sam whispered back.

The next day, after they had put Lyra in the bathtub, he made Marina keep watch on the front porch. Sure enough, around midmorning Marina saw their mother saunter out of the back alley that led to the market.

"Mom's coming!" she screamed, and pounded up the stairs.

Sam picked up the bag of old bath toys and plastic boats he'd gathered, and scattered them around the bathroom. He and Marina scrambled to get Lyra back into Hala Aisha's room, where the old lady got busy combing the mermaid's hair. That always made Lyra quiet and sleepy.

"Surprise!" Mom called as she came in the door. "I brought treats!"

The kids stampeded down the stairs, out of breath and soaking wet.

"Have you guys been messing about in the bathroom all morning?" asked Mom.

"Yup. What did you bring?" asked Marina.

"I'll pour some lemonade!" called Sam, already in the kitchen.

"Didn't Hala Aisha's friend come by?" Mom asked, obviously disappointed. She put the white bakery box on the table, and Marina attacked the knots.

"She went back to her place," said Sam.

"Hala Aisha's with her now," said Marina.

"So she lives in the neighborhood, then?" asked Mom.

"Oh, yes," said Marina. And to prevent any further questions, Sam knocked over the lemonade pitcher.

Mermaid Mission Impossible

Sam and Marina didn't know how to fend off Miss McVitie like they did their mother. Miss McVitie was a bit peculiar. Though she chattered nonstop to the kids when she had the opportunity, she was shy and awkward around other grownups. She rarely showed up when the kids' parents were home.

"I was a nanny once, you know," Sam heard her explain to Dad once. "Far be it from me to intrude on your family time."

But ever since last summer, the first one in which Sam and Marina had looked

after themselves, Miss McVitie seemed to think it her duty to keep an eye on the children when she could. Sam told her that they were quite all right this summer—their aunt was visiting. Still, Miss McVitie would show up at their front door when she got off work, bringing odd things. Once it was a white sweater, much too small for Marina.

"I've made such a sweater for many a wee one," she told Marina.

"Oh. Okay," said Marina. She shook her head and put the sweater in with her dolls' clothes, feeling a deep pity for Miss McVitie. Imagine believing in fairies—and knitting sweaters for them!

Another time Miss McVitie gave them a little silver spoon.

"It's too early to use it now, but the day will come sooner than you think!" she told Sam.

"Uh, thanks," said Sam. He'd tried coffee, and was sure it would be years before he tried it again, even with lots of cream and sugar stirred into it. Anyway, the bowl part of the spoon was too big, and the handle was too short and fat. Sam shoved the spoon to the back of the cutlery drawer and forgot about it.

Saturday arrived, the day Mom usually stayed home to clean the house. But Hala Aisha and the kids had spent so much time tidying up after the mermaid that the house was spotless. Hala Aisha made her a lunch, and Sam and Marina bundled three books into a blanket.

"You're always saying you would love to spend a day in the park by yourself," they told her. "Now's your chance."

"I feel like I'm being gotten rid of," she laughed. But they heard her whistling as she walked down the street.

The moment Mom was out of sight, Miss McVitie came to the door. The kids didn't have an excuse ready and had to invite Miss McVitie in. She handed Hala Aisha a beautifully wrapped parcel, then followed Sam and Marina into the living room, where they waited uncomfortably while Hala Aisha made tea.

"So, what have you named your new arrival?" Miss McVitie asked brightly.

A dead silence fell. *She knows!* thought Marina.

"Uh, Lyra." Sam answered the question in a daze. He was recalling that Miss McVitie's bathroom window was right across from theirs.

"A wee maidie! How wonderful!" cried Miss McVitie, clapping her hands.

"Aren't they always maids?" said Marina, puzzled.

Miss McVitie blushed. "Well, no, dear— look at your brother."

Marina did, and Sam shrugged. Hala Aisha came in with the tea.

"As soon as your wee sister is awake, I would love to see her," said Miss McVitie.

Then Marina laughed out loud. So did Sam. They looked at Hala Aisha. She was grinning and holding up a little yellow bonnet she had just unwrapped.

"Well, it is a joyful occasion," said Miss McVitie, "but if you don't stop laughing so loudly, you'll wake the baby!"

It wasn't so funny the next day, though. Mom was weeding the garden and Marina was upstairs keeping Lyra company. The rest of the family was sitting on the deck, enjoying a cool breeze.

"Has anyone seen my plastic tub?" Mom asked. "Sam? You two haven't been playing with it, have you?"

"No," said Sam. *Not exactly playing*, he added to himself.

Mom looked at him suspiciously, but before she could ask any more questions, Miss McVitie popped her head over the fence.

"Congratulations!" she said.

"For what?" asked Mom.

"For the birth—," Miss McVitie started.

"—day!" shouted Sam. He jumped up and grabbed Hala Aisha's hand, shooting her a pleading look. "It's Hala Aisha's birthday! Happy birthday to you!" he began to sing. Mom, Dad and Miss McVitie looked confused, but no one could resist "Happy Birthday." They joined in.

"And now let's go out for ice cream," said Sam quickly, when they were done. "See you later, Miss McVitie!"

That night in bed, Sam had to admit it. "I don't know how long we can keep this up, what with Miss McVitie and every-thing," he said. "This weekend was a killer. And Hala Aisha's going back to Turkey next week. It will be a lot harder then."

"But what else can we do?" asked Marina.

"Give Lyra to someone else?" suggested Sam reluctantly.

"I couldn't," said Marina.

They pushed the pesky thought out of their minds. But a couple days later it came back. Dad came home early. They were just helping Lyra into the bathtub when they heard the front door bang.

"Hey, kids! Grab your things and let's go swimming!" he called. "Kids?"

"Just a minute, Dad!" Sam called back. He and Marina slammed the bath-room door shut and were standing in front of it when Dad came up.

"Hala Aisha's having a bath," babbled Marina, crossing her fin-gers, "with the radio on. And she's singing along. She's a good singer, don't you think?"

CHAPTER EIGHT

"What program is she listening to?" asked Dad. "Sounds like whale music."

"Uh...CBC?" said Sam.

They had to go swimming then, or Dad would have been suspicious. And it was fun. It felt like forever since they had played outside. They ran all the way to the park. Dad met an old buddy and stood talking while the kids used the swings and the climbing frames. The pool was full of their friends. So, for a while, they forgot what was at home.

But then Marina, zipping off the slide with a huge splash, suddenly thought, *Lyra must miss this*. And Sam, swimming underwater, wondered, *Is this how it feels in the sea?* And in a little while, they didn't want to swim anymore.

For the first time, it was *Dad* who had to be dragged from the pool.

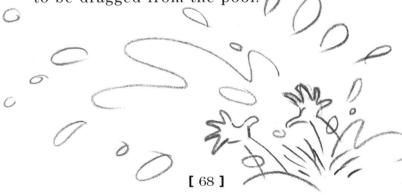

Wanted: Mermaid Sitter

"So, what can we do?" finished Sam. They were in Hala Aisha's room, and Sam had just spilled out all their thoughts and worries.

Hala Aisha nodded her head sympathetically. She said, "Lyra is not a pet. She belongs in the sea."

"But we don't have a sea," said Marina. "We only have a lake! It's big but it's not salty, and it gets very cold in the winter. She'll freeze!" She was close to tears.

"Yes," said Hala Aisha. "By my village, the water is never so cold."

There was a long pause.

"You're going back to Turkey next week," Sam said slowly. "You could take her with you."

"How? In a suitcase?" asked Marina. She looked doubtful.

"No. We'd have to buy her a ticket," said Sam. "But where would we get that kind of money?"

"From this," said Hala Aisha.

She lifted the heavy gold chain she always wore and showed Sam and Marina what hung at the end of it: a jewel that sparkled with the colors of a summer sea. Lyra made a soft bubbling sound.

Sam reached out with one finger to stroke the jewel. "It's the gift your mermaid gave you," he guessed, remembering Hala Aisha's story.

The old woman nodded. Sam saw the determined look on her face.

"You've been thinking about this for a while, haven't you?" he said, and Hala Aisha nodded again. "Why didn't you say something?"

Hala Aisha squeezed Sam's hand. "It's better to think for yourself," she said.

Marina took Hala Aisha's other hand. The skin on top was loose and very soft. "Are you sure, Hala Aisha?" she asked.

The old woman shrugged. "It came from a mermaid. This is a good way to let it go."

They were all quiet for a moment, even the mermaid.

Then the old woman clapped her hands. She smiled at their sad faces. "Cheer up! We have a few days yet." She hoisted herself up. "Right now it is time for bed. We have much to do tomorrow!"

"Dad," Marina asked when he came to kiss them goodnight, "suppose you found some treasure, and you knew it was worth a lot of money. Who would you sell it to?"

"What kind of treasure?" asked Dad.

"Let's say jewels," said Marina.

"Well, you'd take it to a jeweler, I guess. Or maybe an antiques dealer," Dad said. "Of course, first you'd have to make sure it didn't belong to someone else," he added.

"It doesn't," said Marina, without thinking. Then she said quickly, "I mean, it wouldn't. If I found some. Which I didn't." Sam glared at her. "It was just a dream. Boy, I hope I dream that again tonight!" She yawned elaborately.

"Well, just check with your mother before you start digging for treasure in the garden, okay?" Dad warned them. He shook his head. "You two. Goodnight!"

The next day they decided that the first thing they had to do was find a mermaid sitter. It had to be someone steady, someone who could keep a secret. Someone— and this was the toughest part—whose parents were gone all day, but who had just the right kind of grownup nearby, in case of emergencies.

"Someone like Eddie Whan," said Sam. Eddie's parents owned the Asian grocery, and they worked long hours. While they did, Eddie's grandfather looked after him. It seemed perfect.

First they went to the grocery store to

ask if Eddie could come over to play. Then they went to collect him. He was a bit puzzled at the older kids' sudden interest in him, but Eddie had enjoyed having Sam as a reading buddy, and Marina was only one grade ahead of him in school. So he came.

When they showed him Lyra, he beamed.

"Oh, wow. Oh, wow," was all he could say.

They explained the situation and made their plans. Then Eddie played with Lyra while Sam and Marina brought the old baby carriage up from the basement and dusted it off. Marina filled it with her doll collection, just in case Mom asked any awkward questions, and they parked the carriage on the porch.

The next day, they wrapped Lyra up in wet sacking and stuffed her into the carriage. It wasn't easy—she seemed to be getting heavier. They covered her up with blankets and Marina's dolls, to hide her from anyone passing by.

Lyra wanted to look around, which made Sam nervous. But then a car went by and honked at a dog just crossing the road. The dog barked loudly, and Lyra burrowed under the covers in terror. She stayed there until they got to Eddie's place.

"I told my grandfather everything," Eddie told them. "And he said we could use his bathroom."

They settled Lyra, then Eddie called down the stairs to his grandfather. Up he came, step by slow step. He looked at Lyra for a long time, then leaned down to touch her hair. Lyra grabbed his beard and laughed.

Sam and Marina gave Eddie and his grandfather some last-minute instructions. Then they went home to get Hala Aisha.

It was the first time the three of them had gone downtown together. They took the subway, and Hala Aisha was just as interested in sitting in the front as the kids were. Sam had a map, and Marina had the addresses of two antiques dealers and two jewelers. As they walked, they taught Hala Aisha as well as they could about the value of things in Canadian money.

She seemed to catch on quickly. Their conversation with the first shopkeeper took less than two minutes. They were at the second shop a little longer. Hala Aisha browsed for a while in the third shop. She nodded and hummed as she fingered the beautiful knicknacks on display and peered at the jewelry in the dusty cases. Sam and Marina followed her, their hands behind their backs.

At last, looking pleased, Hala Aisha approached the man behind the counter.

He was almost as old as she was. He gasped when he saw her necklace. Sam explained that they wanted to sell it. He turned it over and over in his fingers. He looked at it closely under a bright light and through a telescope-like thing attached to his glasses.

Then he wrote an amount on a piece of paper and pushed it toward Hala Aisha.

Hala Aisha nodded. The man opened a big black book and wrote in it. He carefully tore the page out and handed it to Hala Aisha. Then he beckoned to Sam.

"You'll want to go to my bank with that," he said. "And they'll call me to make sure it's okay." He wrote down the address and explained how to get there. Then he shook their hands.

"I never thought I'd have one of these in my shop," he said. "You tell your grandma it's worth every penny."

The bank teller took them to the manager, and the manager had them wait in his office. He looked alarmed when the children told him they wanted cash. He flinched when Hala Aisha stuffed the fat envelope into her big black bag. He walked with them to the door.

"Please go right to your bank," he begged them in a low voice.

They bought the ticket at the first travel agent they came to.

* * *

Eddie and his grandfather had taken excellent care of Lyra. Eddie had set up a portable stereo in the bathroom for Lyra and put on a tape of whale sounds.

"She sure is loud," Eddie told them. He'd had to turn the music off after the second play-through, when Lyra started singing along. "And she sure eats a lot."

Marina told him how much fish they'd had to eat in order to keep up with Lyra's appetite. Eddie raised his eyebrows. "No wonder you bought so much dried stuff at our store. My parents were kind of wondering," he said.

Eddie's grandfather made Hala Aisha a cup of tea while Sam and Marina put Lyra into the baby carriage and helped Eddie clean up.

"That's funny," said Eddie, as they came downstairs. They could hear conversation in the kitchen.

"What's funny?" asked Sam.

"I guess my grandfather's English is better than I thought," he said.

Marina sent Sam a knowing look.

"See?" she said. "It *is* magic."

Sam shook his head. "People see what they want to see—and when they're really listening, they hear. Hala Aisha and Mr. Whan have something important in common, and that gives them a reason to listen. That's all it is."

It was Marina's turn to shake her head. If a mermaid wasn't magic, what was?

The next day Eddie came over with his grandfather. The old man handed Hala Aisha a sack of mermaid snacks. Then he showed her how to soak the dried squid and cuttle-fish in water till they got soft. Lyra com-plained—loudly. But she ate them.

Eddie made Sam and Marina promise he and his grandfather could come over every day until Hala Aisha took the mermaid home. Sam and Marina didn't mind. It was fun sharing their mermaid. And they were glad that Hala Aisha had made a friend—a *real* one this time.

CHAPTER TEN

Midnight Magic

Then came Saturday again. Mom wanted to stay home to work in the garden, so Lyra had to spend a lot of time in the little tub.

The kids didn't think it was fair for Hala Aisha to keep the mermaid company all the time. So they took turns sitting in Marina's room, reading to Lyra. Though the mermaid didn't speak it, she seemed to understand English just fine.

So, after working through all their picture books and easy chapter books, the kids started in on their mother's collection of favorites. They were in the middle of a story about a girl who discovered she was part fairy and could fly. Lyra loved it. But it was hot up in the bedroom.

Watching them guzzle lemonade in the kitchen, Dad got a little peeved. He had just come home from swimming—all by himself.

"What's wrong with you guys?" he asked. "The Ancient Auntie spends more time outside than you do!"

Sam and Marina glared at him.

"Don't call her that!" they said in unison. Dad held up his hands and backed slowly out of the kitchen.

Then they had a lucky break. Some old friends, who lived north of the city, called to invite Mom and Dad to a pool party. A grownups-only party. It didn't take long for Dad to convince Mom that the kids would be just fine with Hala Aisha.

"Especially now they're all getting on

so well," Marina heard Dad say. "They understand a lot more than they let on, you know. You never hear them talking together, but last night Hala Aisha told me a joke and Sam laughed! I'm positive it was those Turkish lessons."

Marina told Sam to be more careful. "Play dumb for a change, won't you? Or there'll be even more explaining to do," she said.

"It's awfully hard for me," said Sam. "Maybe you can give me lessons?"

Marina swatted him.

As she was packing her things, Mom told the kids she and Dad would be back late. "So don't go to bed too early. Dad and I will want to sleep in tomorrow."

"How late can we stay up?" asked Sam.

"It's up to Hala Aisha," said Mom. "I'm sure she knows what's best."

Hala Aisha *did* know what was best. Because of the heat, the park pool was open until midnight. It took more than an hour to get ready. First they called Eddie. Then they lined the baby carriage with some plastic garbage bags. Next they covered Lyra with Vaseline. Marina had once heard a radio interview with a woman who had swum across Lake Ontario. She had used Vaseline to keep out the cold. Marina thought it would work just as well to keep out chlorine.

At 11:05 they set out. Under her clothes, Hala Aisha was wearing the bathing suit Mom had used when she was expecting Marina. Lyra wore a tank top of Marina's and her tail was covered with towels.

The pool was dimly lit and quiet. Marina was thankful there was no one else in the girls' change room. When she and Hala Aisha staggered out with the slippery Lyra, Eddie and Sam were waiting for them.

They had warned Lyra to be quiet. They had told her to take it easy. Now they laid Lyra on the pool deck, face and arms pointing toward the water. They removed the last towel and pushed her in.

A moment passed, and then her head broke the surface at the far side of the pool. She raised her arms above her head like an Olympic champion and let out a loud squeal.

Sam and Marina let out their breaths, which they had been holding. So did the lifeguard, who'd been uncertain about the new swimmer in the pool. Now that he could see how well she swam, he relaxed. But he blew his whistle crisply.

"No screaming, please," he said.

Sam jumped right into the deep end after Lyra. But Marina was afraid of the deep water. She trudged to the shallow end with Eddie.

"Now Sam will hog Lyra while we're stuck here like babies," she said bitterly.

They paddled around, watching Sam and Lyra play. Marina went down the water slide a couple of times, but it didn't seem as much fun as usual. She felt more and more envious. From time to time, Lyra would come into the shallow end and try to coax Marina and Eddie out.

"Have you tried the deep-water test yet?" Marina asked Eddie, and he shook his head. Marina had tried three times and failed each time.

After a while Sam swam toward them.

"Come on, Marina, take the test! You too, Eddie! Lyra and me'll swim alongside. You can't believe how much fun it is out there with Lyra!"

"Oh, okay," said Marina grumpily.

Sam swam over to tell the lifeguard. Marina and Eddie sidled along the pool edge until they were halfway down the deep end. Sam came back to swim beside Eddie. Lyra bobbed up and down, up and down, on the other side of Marina.

"Ready!" called Sam, and the lifeguard blew his whistle.

Marina pushed off. As usual, after the first six strokes she started to panic. She

couldn't get her head up far enough for a
good deep breath...her arms were getting
tired and her legs were sinking down,
down, down...

Then she felt something nudge her hips
up from below. She opened her eyes. There
was Lyra, gliding along on her back and
smiling up at her. Marina kicked a little
harder and stopped sinking. She turned her
head to one side and got a good, deep

breath. She put her face in the water and pulled hard with her arms. Kick, breathe, pull; kick, breathe, pull. Marina had a rhythm going now, and each time she looked down, Lyra was there. The chlorine smell faded—the sound of splashing, too: it was just Marina and Lyra, flying through the magical blue.

And suddenly she was on the other side of the pool.

"You did it! You did it!" Sam was saying, and Eddie was there, too, panting and triumphant. Lyra was squealing loudly.

The lifeguard blew his whistle. "No screaming, please," he said. "You two can swim in the deep end now."

Sam got a ball. The other kids in the pool drifted toward them as they began to play a game—part tag, part racing, and part water polo. Marina forgot that she'd ever been afraid of the deep water. She jumped right in to tag Sam, then Sam, doing the butterfly all the way, chased her to the water slide. And she wasn't the only one who noticed something different.

Eddie surprised himself by doing a flip

turn. A girl who hated to get her face wet found herself swimming underwater—with her eyes open. A boy who usually stuck to the ladder did a jackknife off the diving board.

"Wow, those swimming lessons really paid off," Sam heard one sleepy grownup say to another. "And that lady with all the hair—who is she? Some kind of swim coach?"

The lifeguard blew his whistle. Swimming was over. Lyra didn't want to leave the pool, so it was a good thing that all the kids wanted to help. In the change room, someone's mother said to Marina, "Your sister's quite a swimmer—you'll be cheering her at the Olympics someday, I'll bet."

Lyra complained all the way home. To calm her, Sam and Marina sang all the Mother Goose songs and lullabies they knew.

Lyra was dozing when they met Miss McVitie, out with her little dog.

"Aren't we up late this evening," she said brightly. She peered into the carriage. "My, she looks so—mature. And a wee bit like you, Sam."

The kids burst out laughing.

"What, er, *jolly* children you are," she said. "Goodnight!" She hurried up her front steps.

The kids were tired after their swim, the laughter, and everything they had to do to clean Lyra up and get her ready for the night. But they were so full of wonder and excitement that they just didn't feel sleepy. So Hala Aisha sang to them—all the Turkish lullabies she knew.

Last Day of a Mermaid

The end of Hala Aisha's visit came too soon.

Hala Aisha had explained to Mom and Dad that her friend would be coming to Turkey with her. Would they drive her to the airport as well? Her friend would meet them here, at the house.

"Well, finally!" Mom said to Sam. "I was beginning to think you two had made her up!"

The day before Hala Aisha was to leave, Sam and Marina brought Lyra over to Eddie's house. She was going to spend the night there—Eddie and his grandfather had it all planned. Marina combed Lyra's hair one last time, then decorated it with every butterfly clip she had, even the jewelled ones. Sam gave her a necklace he'd made himself.

"It doesn't seem like enough," sniffed Marina on the way home.

Sam put his arm around her. "What can you really give to a mermaid?" he asked.

In the morning, they helped Hala Aisha pack.

"All done," she said, getting ready to close the suitcase.

"One more thing, Hala Aisha," said Sam. Marina held up the present they had bought for her: a long-sleeved white shirt with little Canadian flags all over it, and red stockings to go with it. They'd had to borrow a lot of money from Eddie, but it was worth it.

"For when you want to wear something colorful," said Marina.

Hala Aisha had something for the kids, too. To Sam she gave the old picture of herself and her mermaid, in a silver frame. For Marina, there was a silver ring with a stone in it almost the color of the mermaid jewel.

"To remember," she said.

"How could we forget?" said Marina. Suddenly, there were tears in her eyes.

"And not just Lyra, Hala Aisha," said Sam. And he sniffed, because his nose felt so prickly.

Then it was time to go to the airport. Eddie and his grandfather came, pushing a borrowed wheelchair. Inside was Lyra, bundled from head to fins in woolly shawls.

"Mom, Dad, this is Hala Aisha's friend, Mrs....Lyra," said Sam. They all shook hands. Eddie handed over the sports bag he was carrying, full of water bottles and bags of dried shrimp and toasted seaweed.

"Is this all?" asked Dad, as he stuffed it into the trunk.

"Mrs. Lyra travels light," said Sam. "Here, Dad—you take her arms, and I'll take her, um, bottom part."

With Lyra in the back seat, Sam had to sit in the front, so there was no room for Mom. She kissed and hugged Hala Aisha and made sure Marina was buckled in. Just before they pulled away, she leaned in through Dad's window and whispered, "That friend of Auntie is younger than I thought she'd be. But she doesn't seem too well—her hand was so cold, and she smells a bit funny. I hope they'll be all right."

Sam hoped so, too.

All the way to the airport, Marina held Lyra's hand under the shawls, and Hala Aisha's on her other side. When they arrived, they sent Dad to get an airport wheelchair and a luggage cart so that they could say goodbye one last time in private. Hala Aisha took the children's faces in her hands—first Sam's, then Marina's.

"Cheer up!" she whispered. "I have one more surprise for you." They begged her to tell, but she shook her head. "I will write" was all she said.

When they got back, Miss McVitie waved to them from her front porch.

"Bring the baby over any time!" she said.

"What on earth is she talking about?" said Dad.

"She must think you're someone else. You know how she keeps losing her glasses," said Marina. She raised her eyebrows at Sam. They would have some explaining to do later.

"Let's go to the park," suggested Dad.

"Yes!" said Sam. He burst into a run, suddenly feeling as light as a bird.

For the next few days, Sam and Marina enjoyed every boring old summer thing. They played with their friends at the park; they skated up and down the sidewalk; and they complained about having to eat fish—

though secretly they admitted that it just didn't seem that bad anymore. Life went back to normal, except for one thing: Eddie's grandfather had agreed to supervise the kids during the day. Eddie's parents were happy that their son had company. Sam and Marina's parents were happy that there was someone to take their children swimming. And the kids were happy to be able to talk about Lyra because, as time passed, the whole thing started to seem more and more unreal.

Then Hala Aisha's promised letter came. Sam was all ready to read it aloud, but he found he didn't know as much Turkish as he thought he did.

"See?" whispered Marina. "It was mermaid magic!"

Sam scowled and gave the letter to Dad to read.

Dear family,

Thank you so much for a wonderful visit. The journey home was tiring and difficult. The plane was very dry and we were glad we had the bottles. The bus ride from the airport to my village was long and bumpy. We went to the beach as soon as we got home. Lyra was not well by then. Your cousin Erol carried her to the shore and then left us alone to say goodbye. Since then, her health has improved, and she seems to have decided to stay around here. I see her from time to time.

Maybe you would like to see her again, too. Dear children, there was money left over. So Lyra and I hope to see you here next summer!

Love,

Hala Aisha.

"What a strange person that friend of Hala Aisha seems to be," Mom remarked, and then held something up. "How on earth did this baby spoon get in the cutlery drawer?"

"Left over from what? What money? Sam, Marina—what does this mean?" asked Dad.

They were too busy high-fiving to answer.

FIRST FLIGHT READERS

Featuring award-winning authors and illustrators and a fabulous cast of characters, First Flight readers introduce children to the joy of reading.

Short stories with simple sentences and recognizable words for children eager to read. Ideal for sharing with your emergent reader.

High interest stories and language play for developing readers. Slightly longer sentences and words may require a little help.

More complex themes and plots for the independent reader. These stories have short chapters with lively illustrations on each page.

Much longer chapters with black line illustrations interspersed throughout the book for confident, independent readers.

FIRST FLIGHT

Other Books in the First Flight® Series

Fishes in the Ocean
By Richard Thompson and Maggee Spicer
Illustrated by Barbara Hartmann
■ 1-55041-395-3 lb   ■ 1-55041-387-2 pb
■ 1-55041-660-X big book

The Sled and Other Fox and Rabbit Stories
By David McPhail
Illustrated by John O'Connor
■ 1-55041-515-8 lb   ■ 1-55041-517-4 pb

Then and Now
By Richard Thompson
Illustrated by Barbara Hartmann
■ 1-55041-510-7 lb   ■ 1-55041-508-5 pb

There's Music in a Pussycat
By Richard Thompson
Illustrated by Barbara Hartmann
■ 1-55041-511-5 lb   ■ 1-55041-513-1 pb

We'll All Go Sailing
By Richard Thompson and Maggee Spicer
Illustrated by Kim LaFave
■ 1-55041-651-0 pb

FIRST FLIGHT

The Blue Door
By David McPhail
Illustrated by John O'Connor
■ 1-55041-802-5 pb

Alice and the Birthday Giant
By John Green
Illustrated by Maryann Kovalski
■ 1-55041-538-7 lb   ■ 1-55041540-9 pb

Flying Lessons
Written and illustrated by Celia Godkin
■ 1-55041-401-1 lb   ■ 1-55041-399-6 pb

Jingle Bells
Written and illustrated by Maryann Kovalski
■ 1-55041-383-X pb

No Frogs for Dinner
By Frieda Wishinsky
Illustrated by Linda Hendry
■ 1-55041-519-0 lb   ■ 1-55041-521-2 pb

Omar on Ice
Written and illustrated by Maryann Kovalski
■ 1-55041-409-7 lb   ■ 1-55041-407-0 pb

Rain, Rain
Written and illustrated by Maryann Kovalski
■ 1-55041-518-2 lb   ■ 1-55041-520-4 pb
■ 1-55041-659-6 big book

Reading
2
With help

FIRST FLIGHT

Matthew and the Midnight Wrestlers
By Allen Morgan
Illustrated by Michael Martchenko
■ 1-55041-902-1 lb   ■ 1-55041-904-8 pb

Matthew and the Midnight Pirates
By Allen Morgan
Illustrated by Michael Martchenko
■ 1-55041-902-1 lb   ■ 1-55041-904-8 pb

Matthew and the Midnight Firefighter
By Allen Morgan
Illustrated by Michael Martchenko
■ 1-55041-875-0 lb   ■ 1-55041-877-7 pb

Andrew, Catch That Cat!
By Deanne Lee Bingham
Illustrated by Kim LaFave
■ 1-55041-411-9 lb   ■ 1-55041-413-5 pb

Andrew's Magnificent Mountain of Mittens
By Deanne Lee Bingham
Illustrated by Kim LaFave
■ 1-55041-397-X lb   ■ 1-55041-389-9 pb

Ellen's Terrible TV Troubles
By Rachna Gilmore
Illustrated by John Mardon
■ 1-55041-525-5 lb   ■ 1-55041-527-1 pb

Reading
3
Alone

FIRST FLIGHT

Advanced
4
Reading